Name:

Your next
appointment is:

SMILE!

First published 2006 as *Maisy, Charley and the Wobbly Tooth* by Walker Books Ltd
87 Vauxhall Walk, London SE11 5HJ

This edition published 2023

2 4 6 8 10 9 7 5 3 1

© 1990–2023 Lucy Cousins
Lucy Cousins font © 1990–2023 Lucy Cousins

Illustrated in the style of Lucy Cousins by King Rollo Films Ltd

Maisy™. Maisy is a trademark of Walker Books Ltd, London

The right of Lucy Cousins to be identified as author of this work has been
asserted in accordance with the Copyright, Designs and Patents Act 1988.

Printed in China

British Library Cataloguing in Publication Data:
a catalogue record for this book is
available from the British Library

ISBN: 978-1-5295-1262-5

www.walker.co.uk

Maisy Goes to the Dentist

Lucy Cousins

WALKER BOOKS
AND SUBSIDIARIES
LONDON · BOSTON · SYDNEY · AUCKLAND

One day Charley had a wobbly tooth.

He was a little frightened, but Maisy said he should go to see Dr Biteright, the dentist. "He's ever so nice," Maisy said.

Everyone went with Charley.
There was lots to do in the
waiting room.

Charley was beginning to think having a wobbly tooth was OK.

Dr Biteright was really nice, just as Maisy had said.

He showed Charley his special dentist's chair.

It went up ...

down ...

round and round ...

and right back like a bed.

charley had to open his mouth
as wide as he could ...

so Dr Biteright could look inside.

"My, Charley, what a lot of teeth you have!"

But what good teeth.

Dr Biteright
said Charley
shouldn't worry.

The wobbly tooth
was a baby tooth,
ready to fall out.
A new one would
grow in its place.

Then Nurse Sparkle
took an x-ray photo
of Charley's teeth.

Smile, Charley!

And Charley and
Maisy learned
how to brush
their teeth –
up and down,
front and back.

Then Charley had to rinse and spit the mouthwash ...

and rinse and spit again ...

until his teeth were dazzling!

Dr Biteright
gave Charley
a smiley badge
and a book
about teeth ...

and Charley wibbled his wobbly tooth all the way home.

At bedtime, Charley brushed his teeth very carefully... up, down, front and back then...

POP!

Out came the wibbly-wobbly tooth.

So Charley wrapped it in tissue, tucked it under his pillow, and waited ...

for the Tooth Fairy to come!